Santa Claus

ILLUSTRATED BY GILL GUILE
WRITTEN BY DIANE JACKMAN

Brimax Books · Newmarket · England

Santa Claus was polishing his big, black boots. They were so shiny he could see his own smiling face in them.

"I must look my best on Christmas Eve," said Santa. "Even if I am covered in soot by Christmas morning." He pulled on his boots and his red jacket.

"Ready to go!" said Santa.

Mr Holly was Santa's helper.
He was tall and thin and wore
a suit made of holly leaves.
Mr Holly was looking for his hat.
Where could it be? He picked up
Snowflake the cat. There was
his hat! He brushed it quickly
and put it on.
"Ready to go!" said Mr Holly.

Outside, the reindeer were
tossing their heads and
stamping their feet.
They couldn't wait to be off!
This was the most exciting
night of the year. Santa Claus
and Mr Holly began to load
the sleigh with toys and
games. Soon the sleigh was
stacked high.
"Ready to go!" said everyone.

Mr Holly sat next to Santa and looked at the map. At last Santa flicked the reins and the sleigh lifted into the night. There was a full moon and the stars twinkled brightly in the sky. "A perfect Christmas Eve," said Santa Claus. The reindeer nodded and the sleigh bells jingled in the frosty air.

Soon they reached the first house. Santa Claus climbed down the chimney. He read the list pinned to a stocking by the fireplace.

"Mandy would like a teddy and a clock," called Santa up the chimney. Mr Holly searched in the sacks and found the right presents. He handed them down to Santa, who put them in the stocking.

When Santa Claus climbed down Ben's chimney, he fell into an enormous sack stretched across the fireplace. "Oh, my boots and whiskers!" said Santa in surprise. He scrambled out, tangled up in the longest list he had ever seen. "What a greedy boy," said Santa. "If I give him all these presents, some children will have none."

"Pass the sack up to me," said Mr Holly, then he found a sewing box and set to work with needle and cotton. Snip, snip, snip went the scissors. In and out went the needle. At last Mr Holly held up a tiny stocking cut out of the enormous sack. "This should be big enough for just one present," he said.

Then the sleigh landed on the roof of a little crooked cottage. The door twisted one way, the window twisted the other. Even the chimney was twisted, just like a corkscrew. Santa Claus took a deep breath and started to climb down. But at the first twist he got stuck.

"Help! Help!" cried Santa.

Mr Holly tugged. The reindeer tugged. At last Santa popped out of the chimney.

"What shall we do?" he asked. Mr Holly took a fishing rod from the back of the sleigh. He dropped the line down the chimney, then pulled up a yellow stocking.

"Paul would like a watch," said Mr Holly.

Santa filled the stocking and lowered it down the chimney.

They travelled through the night, climbing down chimneys and filling stockings until they came to the last house. Santa found a pair of purple stockings which belonged to Tessa and Tom, who were twins. Mr Holly searched among the sacks. "Santa Claus," called Mr Holly down the chimney, "I am afraid there are no more presents!"

Santa searched the sacks, too. "This has never happened to me before," he said. "Santa Claus can't run out of presents! Whatever shall we do, Mr Holly? Tessa and Tom will wake up to find empty stockings." Santa and Mr Holly sat side by side on the roof and thought and thought.

"What would the twins like for Christmas?" asked Mr Holly. Santa read the list then he clapped his hands in delight. "Of course! Read this, Mr Holly." Mr Holly put on his glasses. "Dear Santa Claus," he read, "our Dad is the local toymaker so we don't need any toys. Could we have a sleigh ride instead, please? From Tessa and Tom."

How Tessa and Tom enjoyed their sleigh ride. They took turns to hold the reins and drove round the town three times. They could see their friends' houses and Grandma's cottage by the lake. At last they landed on their own roof. The twins waved goodbye and jingled the sleigh bells Santa had given them. They would remember this perfect Christmas Eve forever!

Say these words again.

polishing	cottage
buttons	watch
exciting	searched
frosty	delight
clock	forever
enormous	shiny
present	reins